in our time

Annotated and Illustrated

1924 edition

Ernest Hemingway

Annotated and Illustrated
by
A.P. SIMMONS

In Our Time
Annotated and Illustrated

A.P. Simmons

Printed in the United States of America
First Printing 2021
First Edition 2021

ISBN 9798454735791

Edited By: A.P. Simmons
Cover Design By: A.P. Simmons

acknowledgments

Ernest Hemingway was 24 years old when the first edition of *in our time* was published in 1924. This book was his second published book, following *Three Stories and Ten Poems*. I did not edit any of the text. I believe Mr. Hemingway's diction is modern enough to be understood as it was originally published. A longer second edition was published in 1925, and a third edition in 1930, which added the story *On the Quai at Smyrna*.

I wanted to accomplish two things with this annotated and illustrated edition. One, where appropriate, I wanted to provide photos or pictures that were from that era. None of us today have memories of images from that time, and a photograph or picture may help provide better context for the modern reader. Two, I wanted to provide some explanations of events, locations, names, or general observations to the modern reader. In 1924 the average reader may have understood what oilcloth was. That is probably no longer the case, so annotations of that nature will hopefully enrich your understanding of the stories.

The cover was based on an unattributed photo from the Ernest Hemingway Photograph Collection in the John F. Kennedy Presidential Library and Museum, Boston. The photo shows the 19-year-old Hemingway recovering from shrapnel wounds in a Milan hospital, 1918.

English Book of Common Prayer

"Give peace **in our time**, O Lord"

Table of Contents

chapter 1

Photo: Troops of the 10th Battalion Marching, circa 1915

Everybody was drunk. The whole battery was drunk going along the road in the dark. We were going to the Champagne[1]. The lieutenant kept riding his horse out into the fields and saying to him, "I'm drunk, I tell you, mon vieux. Oh, I am so soused." We went along the road all

---

[1] Hemingway is describing a march to the Champagne region of France in World War I.

night in the dark and the adjutant kept riding up alongside my kitchen and saying, "You must put it out. It is dangerous. It will be observed." We were fifty kilometers from the front but the adjutant worried about the fire in my kitchen. It was funny going along that road. That was when I was a kitchen corporal.[2]

---

[2] This story is likely inspired by Chink Dorman-Smith, Hemingway's friend, who was at the Battle of Mons. Hemingway served in the Italian Front as a Red Cross ambulance driver in World War I.

chapter 2

Photo: Bullfighting in Madrid, Spain

Photo via   https://www.goodfreephotos.com/cache/spain/madrid/bullfighting-in-madrid-spain.jpg

The first matador got the horn through his sword hand and the crowd hooted him out[3]. The second matador slipped and the bull caught him through the belly and he hung on to the horn with one hand and held the other tight against the place, and the bull rammed him wham against the wall and the horn came out, and he lay in the sand, and then got

---

[3] Hemingway is describing a bullfight likely inspired by conversation with his friend, Mike Strater.

up like crazy drunk and tried to slug the men carrying him away and yelled for his sword but he fainted. The kid came out and had to kill five bulls because you can't have more than three matadors, and the last bull he was so tired he couldn't get the sword in. He couldn't hardly lift his arm. He tried five times and the crowd was quiet because it was a good bull and it looked like him or the bull and then he finally made it. He sat down in the sand and puked and they held a cape over him while the crowd hollered and threw things down into the bull ring[4].

---

[4] At this early point in his career Hemingway was already writing about two topics that involved great bravery and death: war and bullfighting.

chapter 3

Photo: Armenian refugees, 1915

Minarets stuck up in the rain out of Adrianople[5] across the mud flats. The carts were jammed for thirty miles along the Karagatch road. Water buffalo and cattle were hauling carts through the mud. No end and no beginning. Just carts loaded with everything they owned. The old men and women, soaked through, walked along keeping the cattle moving. The Maritza was running yellow almost up to the bridge. Carts were jammed solid on the bridge with camels bobbing along through them. Greek cavalry herded along

---

[5] Adrianople is a city in northwest Turkey, on the European continent.

the procession. Women and kids were in the carts crouched with mattresses, mirrors, sewing machines, bundles. There was a woman having a kid with a young girl holding a blanket over her and crying. Scared sick looking at it. It rained all through the evacuation[6].

---

[6] Hemingway witnessed events that inspired the stories of the Greco-Turkish War. He was an in-theater reporter, on assignment for The Toronto Star in 1922.

chapter 4

Photo: 4ᵗʰ Dragoon Guards at Mons, 1914

We were in a garden at Mons. Young Buckley came in with his patrol from across the river. The first German I saw climbed up over the garden wall. We waited till he got one leg over and then potted[7] him. He had so much equipment on and looked awfully surprised and fell down into the garden. Then three more came over further down the wall. We shot them. They all came just like that[8].

---

[7] "Potted" was a term to describe killing someone. They were buried in the earth. Like a potted plant.

[8] Note that Hemingway does not embellish war experiences. But his cold, lean writing style was something that veterans could appreciate.

chapter 5

THOUSANDS DIE IN HAND-TO-HAND BATTLE
GERMAN PONTOON COMPANIES CROSS MONS-CONDE' CANAL

ALLIES TRY TO TAKE
INVADERS' TRENCHES

Illustration from the Washington Times, September 20, 1914.

It was a frightfully hot day. We'd jammed an absolutely perfect barricade across the bridge. It was simply priceless. A big old wrought iron grating from the front of a house. Too heavy to lift and you could shoot through it and they would have to climb over it. It was absolutely topping[9]. They tried to get over it, and we potted them from forty yards. They rushed it, and officers came out alone and worked on it. It was an absolutely perfect obstacle. Their

---

[9] Note the appreciation of a seemingly simple accomplishment. But it saved lives, which was a source of happiness for the defenders. War veterans could relate to the feelings.

officers were very fine. We were frightfully put out when we heard the flank had gone, and we had to fall back[10].

---

[10] Mons, France: the 1914 battle raged over the Nimy bridge. This was the first major engagement of the British in the war.

chapter 6

They shot the six cabinet ministers at half-past six in the morning against the wall of a hospital[11]. There were pools of water in the courtyard. There were wet dead leaves on the paving of the courtyard. It rained hard. All the shutters of the hospital were nailed shut. One of the ministers was sick with typhoid. Two soldiers carried him downstairs and out into the rain. They tried to hold him up against the wall but he sat down in a puddle of water. The other five stood very quietly against the wall. Finally the officer told the soldiers it was no good trying to make him stand up. When they fired the first volley he was sitting down in the water with his head on his knees.

---

[11] Hemingway provides another story, based on real events, from the Greco-Turkish War.

chapter 7

Photo of Combles France, 1916

Nick[12] sat against the wall of the church where they had dragged him to be clear of machine gun fire in the street. Both legs stuck out awkwardly. He had been hit in the spine[13]. His face was sweaty and dirty. The sun shone on his face. The day was very hot. Rinaldi, big backed, his

---

[12] Nick, believed to be Nick Adams, is a character that is supposedly Hemingway's alter ego. Nick will be a character that Hemingway revisits throughout his career.
[13] Hemingway himself was injured in the Great War. He received shrapnel wounds while serving in Italy.

equipment sprawling, lay face downward against the wall. Nick looked straight ahead brilliantly. The pink wall of the house opposite had fallen out from the roof, and an iron bedstead hung twisted toward the street. Two Austrian dead lay in the rubble in the shade of the house. Up the street were other dead. Things were getting forward in the town. It was going well. Stretcher bearers would be along any time now. Nick turned his head carefully and looked down at Rinaldi. "Senta Rinaldi. Senta. You and me we've made a separate peace." Rinaldi lay still in the sun breathing with difficulty. "Not patriots." Nick turned his head carefully away smiling sweatily. Rinaldi was a disappointing audience.

chapter 8

Photo of artillery explosion in World War I, circa 1916

While the bombardment[14] was knocking the trench to pieces at Fossalta[15], he lay very flat and sweated and prayed oh jesus christ get me out of here. Dear jesus please get me out. Christ please please please christ. If you'll only keep me from getting killed I'll do anything you say. I believe in you and I'll tell everyone in the world that you are the only

---

[14] Over half the injuries in World War I were caused by artillery.
[15] Hemingway spent most of his time serving in Italy in and around the villages of Fornaci and Fossalta.

thing that matters. Please please dear jesus[16]. The shelling moved further up the line[17]. We went to work on the trench and in the morning the sun came up and the day was hot and muggy and cheerful and quiet. The next night back at Mestre[18] he did not tell the girl he went upstairs with at the Villa Rossa about Jesus. And he never told anybody.

---

[16] Most people who have undergone a traumatic threat to their life can relate to this soldier's appeal to God to get through it. Mark Twain also wrote about this phenomenon in his novel *Roughing It*.
[17] Soldiers could identify the type of artillery based on the sounds they made. To this day, artillery fire on your position is considered one of the most terrifying experiences in war.
[18] Mestre is a borough of Venice.

chapter 9

At two o'clock in the morning two Hungarians got into a cigar store at Fifteenth Street and Grand Avenue. Drevitts and Boyle drove up from the Fifteenth Street police station in a Ford. The Hungarians were backing their wagon[19] out of an alley. Boyle shot one off the seat of the wagon and one out of the wagon box. Drevetts got frightened when he found they were both dead. Hell Jimmy, he said, you oughtn't to have done it. There's liable to be a hell of a lot of trouble[20].

—They're crooks ain't they? said Boyle. They're wops[21] ain't they? Who the hell is going to make any trouble?

—That's all right maybe this time, said Drevitts, but how did you know they were wops when you bumped them?

Wops, said Boyle, I can tell wops a mile off.

---

[19] Horses were in wide use during World War I.
[20] Hemingway is relating the brutality of total war. War crimes are seldom prosecuted, particularly by the victors.
[21] "Wop" was a pejorative term used in that era to describe Italians or other southern Europeans.

chapter 10

Photo of Duomo Plaza, Milan

Photo via   https://www.goodfreephotos.com/cache/italy/milan/plaza-duomo.jpg

One hot evening in Milan they carried him up onto the roof and he could look out over the top of the town. There were chimney swifts in the sky. After a while it got dark and the searchlights came out. The others went down and took the bottles with them. He and Ag[22] could hear them below on the balcony. Ag sat on the bed. She was cool and fresh in the hot night.

---

[22] In this story, "Ag" is the nurse tending to the soldier.

Ag stayed on night duty for three months. They were glad to let her. When they operated on him she prepared him for the operating table, and they had a joke about friend or enema. He went under the anæsthetic holding tight on to himself so that he would not blab about anything during the silly, talky time. After he got on crutches[23] he used to take the temperature so Ag would not have to get up from the bed. There were only a few patients, and they all knew about it. They all liked Ag. As he walked back along the halls he thought of Ag in his bed.

Before he went back to the front they went into the Duomo and prayed. It was dim and quiet, and there were other people praying. They wanted to get married, but there was not enough time for the banns, and neither of them had birth certificates. They felt as though they were married, but they wanted everyone to knew about it, and to make it so they could not lose it.

Ag wrote him many letters that he never got until after the armistice. Fifteen came in a bunch and he sorted them by the dates and read them all straight through. They were

---

[23] Hemingway recovered from his shrapnel wounds in an army hospital in Milan.

about the hospital, and how much she loved him and how it was impossible to get along without him and how terrible it was missing him at night[24].

After the armistice they agreed he should go home to get a job so they might be married. Ag would not come home until he had a good job and could come to New York to meet her. It was understood he would not drink, and he did not want to see his friends or anyone in the States. Only to get a job and be married. On the train from Padova to Milan they quarrelled about her not being willing to come home at once. When they had to say good-bye in the station at Padova they kissed good-bye, but were not finished with the quarrel. He felt sick about saying good-bye like that.

He went to America on a boat from Genoa. Ag went back to Torre di Mosta to open a hospital. It was lonely and rainy there, and there was a battalion of arditi quartered in the town. Living in the muddy, rainy town in the winter the major of the battalion made love to Ag, and she had never known Italians before, and finally wrote a letter to the States that theirs had been only a boy and girl affair. She was sorry, and she knew he would probably not be able to understand, but might some day forgive her, and be

---

[24] Hemingway fell in love with a nurse who eventually left him for an Italian soldier.

grateful to her, and she expected, absolutely unexpectedly, to be married in the spring. She loved him as always, but she realized now it was only a boy and girl love. She hoped he would have a great career, and believed in him absolutely. She knew it was for the best.

The Major did not marry her in the spring, or any other time. Ag never got an answer to her letter to Chicago about it. A short time after he contracted gonorrhea from a sales girl from The Fair riding in a taxicab through Lincoln Park.

chapter 11

Photo of railroad view

Photo via   https://www.goodfreephotos.com/cache/other-landscapes/fall-railroad-tracks-and-leaves-in-the-forest.jpg

In 1919 he was travelling on the railroads in Italy carrying a square of oilcloth[25] from the headquarters of the party written in indelible pencil and saying here was a comrade who had suffered very much under the whites in Budapest[26] and requesting comrades to aid him in any way.

---

[25] "Oilcloth" was a linen cloth with a coating of boiled linseed oil to make it waterproof. It was used as an outer waterproof layer for clothing and luggage.
[26] The "whites in Budapest" were soldiers used to crush anyone supportive of the opposition, Hungary's Soviet republic (reds).

He used this instead of a ticket. He was very shy and quite young and the train men passed him on from one crew to another. He had no money, and they fed him behind the counter in railway eating houses.

He was delighted with Italy. It was a beautiful country he said. The people were all kind. He had been in many towns, walked much and seen many pictures. Giotto, Masaccio, and Piero della Francesca he bought reproductions of and carried them wrapped in a copy of Avanti. Mantegna he did not like.

He reported at Bologna, and I took him with me up into the Romagna where it was necessary I go to see a man. We had a good trip together. It was early September and the country was pleasant. He was a Magyar, a very nice boy and very shy. Horthy's men[27] had done some bad things to him. He talked about it a little. In spite of Italy, he believed altogether in the world revolution.

—But how is the movement going in Italy? he asked.

---

[27] Horthy led a conservative and antisemitic government beginning in 1920. "Horthy's men" described his police and soldier support.

—Very badly, I said.

—But it will go better, he said. You have everything here. It is the one country that everyone is sure of. It will be the starting point of everything.

At Bologna he said good-bye to us to go on the train to Milano and then to Aosta to walk over the pass into Switzerland. I spoke to him about the Mantegnas in Milano. No, he said, very shyly, he did not like Mantegna. I wrote out for him where to eat in Milano and the addresses of comrades. He thanked me very much, but his mind was already looking forward to walking over the pass. He was very eager to walk over the pass while the weather held good. The last I heard of him the Swiss had him in jail near Sion.

chapter 12

They whack whacked the white horse on the legs and he knee-ed himself up. The picador[28] twisted the stirrups straight and pulled and hauled up into the saddle. The horse's entrails hung down in a blue bunch and swung backward and forward as he began to canter, the monos whacking him on the back of his legs with the rods. He cantered jerkily along the barrera[29]. He stopped stiff and one of the monos held his bridle and walked him forward. The picador kicked in his spurs, leaned forward and shook his lance at the bull. Blood pumped regularly from between the horse's front legs. He was nervously wobbly. The bull could not make up his mind to charge.

---

[28] Picadors in a bullfight frequently ride horses. Their role is to tire the bull's neck muscles. The horses are sometimes killed or injured in bullfighting. Horse injuries were more common in Hemingway's time, before the horses were provided a protection blanket.
[29] The "barrera" is the wooden fence or barrier surrounding the bullring.

chapter 13

The crowd shouted all the time and threw pieces of bread down into the ring, then cushions and leather wine bottles, keeping up whistling and yelling. Finally the bull was too tired from so much bad sticking and folded his knees and lay down and one of the cuadrilla[30] leaned out over his neck and killed him with the puntillo.[31] The crowd came over the barrera and around the torero[32] and two men grabbed him and held him and some one cut off his pigtail and was waving it and a kid grabbed it and ran away with it. Afterwards I saw him at the café. He was very short with a brown face and quite drunk and he said after all it has happened before like that. I am not really a good bull fighter.

---

[30] A "cuadrilla" is an assistant of the matador in a bullfight.
[31] A "puntillo" is a dagger or sword used to deliver the killing blow to a bull.
[32] The "torero" becomes a matador when he kills the bull.

chapter 14

If it happened right down close in front of you, you could see Villalta[33] snarl at the bull and curse him, and when the bull charged he swung back firmly like an oak when the wind hits it, his legs tight together, the muleta trailing and the sword following the curve behind. Then he cursed the bull, flopped the muleta at him, and swung back from the charge his feet firm, the muleta curving and each swing the crowd roaring.

When he started to kill it was all in the same rush. The bull looking at him straight in front, hating. He drew out the sword from the folds of the muleta and sighted with the same movement and called to the bull, Toro! Toro! and the bull charged and Villalta charged and just for a moment they became one. Villalta became one with the bull and then it was over. Villalta standing straight and the red kilt of the sword sticking out dully between the bull's shoulders. Villalta, his hand up at the crowd and the bull roaring blood, looking straight at Villalta and his legs caving.

---

[33] "Villalta" is Nicanor Villalta, a famous Spanish bullfighter and a hero of Hemingway.

chapter 15

I heard the drums coming down the street and then the fifes and the pipes and then they came around the corner, all dancing. The street full of them. Maera[34] saw him and then I saw him. When they stopped the music for the crouch he hunched down in the street with them all and when they started it again he jumped up and went dancing down the street with them. He was drunk all right.

You go down after him, said Maera, he hates me.

So I went down and caught up with them and grabbed him while he was crouched down waiting for the music to break loose and said, Come on Luis[35]. For Christ sake you've got bulls this afternoon. He didn't listen to me, he was listening so hard for the music to start.

I said, Don't be a damn fool Luis. Come on back to the hotel.

---

[34] Maera is a bullfighter.
[35] Luis is another bullfighter.

Then the music started up again and he jumped up and twisted away from me and started dancing. I grabbed his arm and he pulled loose and said, Oh leave me alone. You're not my father.

I went back to the hotel and Maera was on the balcony looking out to see if I'd be bringing him back. He went inside when he saw me and came downstairs disgusted.

Well, I said, after all he's just an ignorant Mexican savage.

Yes, Maera said, and who will kill his bulls after he gets a cogida?

We, I suppose, I said.

Yes, we, said Maera. We kills the savages' bulls, and the drunkards' bulls, and the riau-riau dancers' bulls. Yes. We kill them. We kill them all right. Yes. Yes. Yes.

chapter 16

Maera lay still, his head on his arms, his face in the sand. He felt warm and sticky from the bleeding. Each time he felt the horn coming. Sometimes the bull only bumped him with his head. Once the horn went all the way through him and he felt it go into the sand. Someone had the bull by the tail. They were swearing at him and flopping the cape in his face. Then the bull was gone. Some men picked Maera up and started to run with him toward the barriers through the gate out the passage way around under the grand stand to the infirmary. They laid Maera down on a cot and one of the men went out for the doctor. The others stood around. The doctor came running from the corral where he had been sewing up picador horses. He had to stop and wash his hands. There was a great shouting going on in the grandstand overhead. Maera wanted to say something and found he could not talk. Maera felt everything getting larger and larger and then smaller and smaller. Then it got larger and larger and larger and then smaller and smaller. Then everything commenced to run faster and faster as when they speed up a cinematograph film. Then he was dead.

chapter 17

Photo of Sam Cardinelli, circa 1921

They hanged Sam Cardinella[36] at six o'clock in the morning in the corridor of the county jail.[37] The corridor was high and narrow with tiers of cells on either side. All the cells were occupied. The men had been brought in for the hanging. Five men sentenced to be hanged were in the five top cells. Three of the men to be hanged were negroes[38]. They were very frightened. One of the white men sat on

---

[36] Sam Cardinella was a real person. His actual name was Samuele Cardinelli, although he was born Salvatore Cardinella. He was a mobster in Chicago.
[37] He was executed by hanging on Apr 15, 1921 for the 1919 murder of saloon owner Andrew P. Bowman.
[38] In the 1920's, African-Americans were often referred to as "negroes."

his cot with his head in his hands. The other lay flat on his cot with a blanket wrapped around his head.

They came out onto the gallows through a door in the wall. There were six or seven of them including two priests. They were carrying Sam Cardinella. He had been like that since about four o'clock in the morning.

While they were strapping his legs together two guards held him up and the two priests were whispering to him. "Be a man, my son," said one priest. When they came toward him with the cap to go over his head Sam Cardinella lost control of his sphincter muscle. The guards who had been holding him up dropped him. They were both disgusted. "How about a chair, Will?" asked one of the guards, "Better get one," said a man in a derby hat.

When they all stepped back on the scaffolding back of the drop, which was very heavy, built of oak and steel and swung on ball bearings, Sam Cardinella was left sitting there strapped tight, the younger of the two priests kneeling beside the chair[39]. The priest skipped back onto the scaffolding just before the drop fell.

---

[39] He was hung strapped into a chair.

chapter 18

The king was working in the garden. He seemed very glad to see me[40]. We walked through the garden. This is the queen, he said. She was clipping a rose bush. Oh how do you do, she said. We sat down at a table under a big tree and the king ordered whiskey and soda. We have good whiskey anyway, he said. The revolutionary committee, he told me, would not allow him to go outside the palace grounds. Plastiras[41] is a very good man I believe, he said, but frightfully difficult. I think he did right though shooting those chaps. If Kerensky[42] had shot a few men things might have been altogether different. Of course the great thing in this sort of an affair is not to be shot oneself!

---

[40] Many European royal kingdoms were overthrown during and after World War I.

[41] Nikolaos Plastiras was a three-time prime minister of Greece. As a soldier and general he was known for his bravery.

[42] Alexander Kerensky was a politician in the Russian Revolution of 1917. His government was overthrown by Lenin and the Bolsheviks.

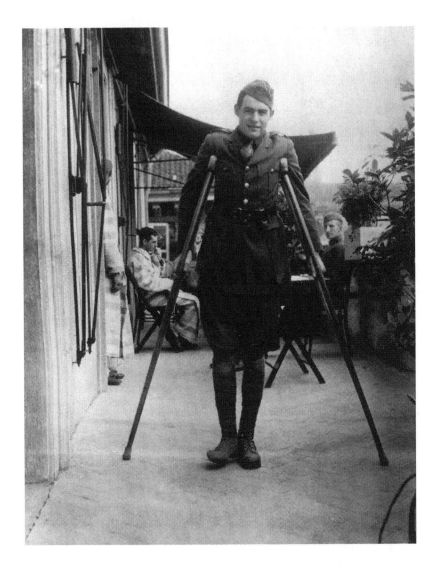

Unattributed photo of 19-year-old Ernest Hemingway in a Milan hospital, 1918

Ernest Hemingway Photograph Collection, John F. Kennedy Presidential Library and Museum, Boston

More by A.P. Simmons

Please visit the website of A.P. Simmons for this and other books!

https://www.apsimmons.com/

Made in the USA
Columbia, SC
13 May 2024

35629715R00028